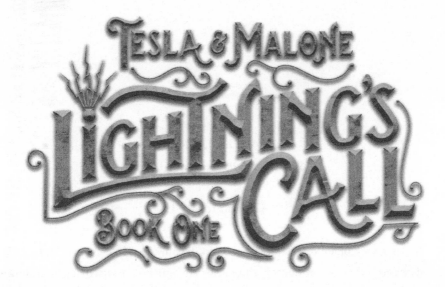

Lightning's Call
By Vincent J. LaRosa
Copyright © 2015 Vincent J. LaRosa.

ISBN: 978-0-9966813-2-2

Interior Formatting by Tugboat Design
Cover Art by Adam Baker
Developmental Editing by Shen Hart
Copy Editing by Angela DiOrio

Visit me at www.vincelarosa.com

For Angela D.
Who gave me support and encouragement.
Thank you for always being there.

A special thanks to my beta readers:
John H., Dan M., & Antonio G.
Thanks, brothers!

ONE

Present Day, Friday - June 6th, 1884.

The force of the scream ripped him from nightmare plagued sleep. Abstract images and colors swirled into his kaleidoscopic view only to be torn away by an unseen hand. He thrashed the bedclothes, twisting the finely made sheets around his naked body. Awareness returned like a shot of old man Grant's devil moonshine to the back of his throat - intense and jolting. He coughed, wiped an unsteady hand at his dripping forehead and shakily sat up.

"Another nightmare, dear one?" A calm, soothing female voice spoke to him from the other side of the room. She inhaled, then slowly expelled a breath. "The same one, again?"

Denis Malone heaved a sigh and massaged his temples. "Yea." He grunted and coughed up mucous. "Same as last week." His handkerchief was on the nightstand next to the money he paid her in tribute. He grabbed the cloth and spit.

"Classy." Amusement tinged the cool, husky female voice. Her dress rustled as she crossed her legs before settling in her chair with one toe tapping the air languidly.

The voice in the corner belonged to Victoria. They were in her bedroom suite, a warm and comforting feminine haven away from the noise, dirt, and chaos of the city outside. A refuge for Denis. A quiet place to forget and feel good.

She sat wrapped in an elegant robe, fur trimmed and open at the throat. The swell of her breasts strained against the thin fabric of their confinement. Rose tinted flesh peeked out from the V made by the robe and twin mounds swelled as she took a slow drag on her cigarette.

Her pale green eyes were cool as she regarded him quietly. She held her toke, then let out another slow breath. "Your nightmares are increasing in frequency, my dear." A thin stream of smoke escaped her gently flared nostrils. She tapped the cigarette out in the sea shell she used as an ashtray and stood up stretching. The robe fell open, her breasts finally winning the battle against confinement. Firm and full, they swayed with her movement.

Unconcerned she walked over to the bedside.

Denis had extricated himself from the clutches of the dream damp bed sheets and now sat hunched on the edge of the bed, head in hands.

"I know. It's every week now." He looked over at her and shook his head. "Used to be only a coupla times a year." He rubbed at the back of his neck and sat up. "And these damn headaches." He ran a hand over a shaved head that throbbed with each pound of his heart. His spine tingled again. Just like when he was a kid, he suddenly recalled. He struggled to find a connection.

Not again. Why now?

Victoria made a sympathetic sound and put her arm across his shoulders, drawing him close to her. He leaned in, allowing himself to be comforted, and breathed in her heady perfume. Roses. He loved when she wore that one for him. He wished he could visit her more often.

She rested her chin on his shoulder and nibbled his ear. "What can I do, love?" Her breath was hot on his skin.

He laughed ruefully. "If it were only that easy." He turned his head and looked into her eyes. "Being here and seeing you helps. The rest is for me to deal with." He kissed her nose gently. "I'll be okay, Vicky. The Malones are fighters." He made a fist and chucked her under the chin lightly.

She laughed and grabbed his hand. "Well, you are my favorite client, my Denis."

He looked at her archly, his eyebrow raised. "Oh yea?"

"Yea." She squeezed his hand, kissed his cheek and stood up, hands on hips. "Let's get you dressed. Don't you have to be in work soon?" She looked pointedly at the clock on the mantel above the fireplace.

He groaned and stood up as well, slapping her on the backside as he searched for his discarded clothes. "Right, as usual." He smiled as he noticed his suit folded neatly over the armchair by the fireplace. "You're the best, Vicky."

Vicky snorted and busied herself at her dressing table. She sat with her head to one side and pulled a pearl handled comb through her thick red mane of hair.

Denis dressed slowly, thinking of the day ahead of him. He suddenly recalled his promise of lunch with John Hawthorne, his friend from The New York Times. He tucked his white shirt into his trousers and snapped his suspenders into place. He winced at the pain in his shoulders.

"Will I see you again later this week, dear one?" Vicky looked at him in the mirror. She ran the comb down the length of her hair and out, then delicately pulled the stray hairs from the teeth of the comb. She flicked hair onto the floor and resumed. "I do believe I am free this Thursday."

Denis sat on the edge of the armchair pulling on his boots. He looked up. "Maybe. I want to but this week's going to be hell, I'm thinking."

He thought that something felt off within him. No. That wasn't right. If he was honest he would say that what he was feeling came from outside himself. A tension, a dread, was in the air that he'd never felt before. The aftershocks of his own unsettled dreams, or something more? He shook his head like a dog shaking water from its fur.

Lately, he felt heavy under this weight of living. He suppressed a sigh, brow steepled slightly, and settled his jaw.

Push it down, as always.

Vicky had stopped her combing and was watching him from the mirror with concern pooling in her eyes. She turned around, her hands twisting around the delicate handle. "Denis, dear, are you sure you're well? You seem - distant - more so than usual. Last night was lovely, but I could sense something not quite right with you."

Denis shrugged into his jacket and pocketed his billfold and pocket watch. He eyed Vicky for a moment. What could he say to that? He sighed. "I'll be fine, my dear. It's those nightmares, they're draining me that's all, making me tired." He gave her a lopsided smile. "Like I said, we Malones—"

"Are fighters." Vicky finished his sentence and sighed. "I know, I know." She shook her head and rose from her seat. "Be careful out there, dear one."

Denis grabbed her in a rough embrace, lifting her and twirling her around. "One of these days, I'm gonna marry you, Victoria!"

Her smile was radiant and tinged with regret. A look of pain passed her face so swiftly as to hardly register. Her eyes tightened yet she laughed and grabbed his mouth in one hand and pinched. "Don't make promises you cannot keep Denis Malone!" She said fiercely, pinning him with smoldering green eyes.

"I mean it," he struggled to say through puckered lips. He pulled his head back, grinning. "I mean it!" He squeezed her hand and then brought it to his mouth, kissing her knuckles lightly. "Enjoy your own day too, my Vicky." He gave her one last squeeze and turned away.

Victoria stood straight and silent for some time watching the door, feeling the weight of his presence still in the room. She smiled sadly and turned back to start her day.

She hoped he would be okay.

Flickering candlelight struggled against the dark, slinking shadows of the damp basement stone floor in the crumbling corner brownstone on Manhattan Island.

Somewhere water dripped. The air was thick and moist. Shadows danced around the black robed figure kneeling silent on the floor before a crude stone altar, its slick surface reflecting back the feeble light as candle wax dripped slowly down the two pillar candles placed on either end of the basalt stone. A small figurine, carved from some blackish green stone, sat between them. On the floor in front of the altar was a small brass bowl, the red liquid inside glowed slightly, the surface rippling faintly as if disturbed from within.

A low hiss escaped the emptiness within the hood.

He is here. I sense his presence on the island. Not far.

Slowly, the figure raised its arms up high in supplication to the sky. A low guttural chanting issued forth, sharp and urgent as it pushed against the moist air, thrusting back the curtain of aether.

The red liquid began to bubble and froth, as small wisps of steam curled upward. The figure leaned forward slightly, its chanting increased in volume and reverberated around the small stone basement. The sound turned back onto itself with a strange harmonic cadence that seemed almost musical.

The chant, echoing around the room, took on an urgent commanding tone that split the air. Dust from the ceiling sifted down like misting rain as the foundation of the house vibrated with energy.

Loose papers fluttered as if alive. Candle light burned out in a sudden flash of blue fire and was extinguished. Something had arrived - from beyond, from outside.

The warm, full breeze, still carrying with it the sharpness of the ocean, tugged at the bottom of Niko's canvas long-coat, sending the tails snapping against his calves. Like the eager wind, he felt alive with raw energy and was eager to get moving.

He was standing on the ready level of the steamer, the S.S. City of Richmond, as it chugged its way into the vast expanse of the harbor. Ahead, the Hudson River heaved and rolled heavily as she emptied herself into the bay. Gulls cried their lonely call and swooped in low over the choppy waters. On their port side, the steamer chugged past Bedloe's Island, and the newly financed Statue of Liberty pedestal. Niko had read that the grand statue herself, a gift to the people of America from France, had arrived in parts. Once complete, a marvel indeed.

He smiled to himself and lowered a worn-down cloth rucksack consisting of a change of clothes, a few toiletries, his papers, and a few coins. Everything he owned in this world, on his back.

Well, not everything.

His smile widened as he shifted his other shoulder and adjusted the leather strap of the long, carrying case. He patted the pine-wood affectionately.

One of his first inventions.

His other two were hidden within the leather snap cases nestled on his belt. Niko pushed his dark goggles further back onto his head and leaned against the railing. He grasped the rust pitted iron with his large, calloused hands and gazed out across the water to the rising buildings that made up the island of Manhattan. The wind ruffled his black hair and he squinted, taking in those tall buildings outlined against the sky. What grand designs of humanity there existed in this new world.

Finally, he had arrived.

A momentary cloud of despair hovered over his thoughts. The bright sunlight felt sinister and the clear sky a deception.

He feared his new equipment would be put to use very soon

The ship's starboard horn blasted and shattered the air, upsetting the gulls and announcing its final approach to the harbor master. Niko watched as crew members scurried about the forward deck, under the stern eye of the ship's quartermaster, each attending to his duty.

The steamer rocked in the waves washing back from the dock. He took a breath and felt the bump of the side cushions absorbing the force as the ship made its berth. Somewhere a whistle blew a trilling low to high note. Not far from where he stood, a crew member released the catch on the gate to the gangway.

Niko checked over his gear one final time, adjusting a strap here and a cinch there, and squared his tense shoulders. Around him other passengers made their own last minute preparations as they all queued to disembark.

With a scrape and rattle of chains, the gangplank was made fast as it was run down to the worn pilings of the boardwalk by a pair of surly looking dock workers dressed in faded, oil stained dockers and ratty shirts. The plank fell into place off balance causing one to let out a yelp and curse. His buddy barked a derisive laugh and lifted the unruly plank, shifting it back into place. He waved up at Niko impatiently.

Smiling tolerantly, he nervously adjusted the dark goggles on his forehead and with one hand grasping the shaky railing, stepped out onto the gangway and began to descend.

Just a few more feet and I will be on American soil! His stomach was flip flopping and his palms began to sweat. He resisted the urge to count the riveted seams in the plank and kept his eyes straight ahead. His smile turned downward a bit as he thought how some things from childhood never change.

Niko finished the last few feet and stepped onto the worn and splintered dock of Castle Clinton. He paused a moment to smile at the two workers. He hoisted his shoulder strap and held out his hand enthusiastically.

"Hello—" he started to greet them.

The crew member looked at him as if he had two heads. He eyed

Niko's garb - long coat, equipment belt, pine box slung over his shoulder, and shock of hair sticking up through the straps of the goggles. He shook his head disgustedly. "Keep it moving, boyo - right over there, ya gotta see the immigration officer!" With a grimy finger, he pointed over to the gated exit nestled in next to a large warehouse structure. His accented English put him as Irishman - an immigrant himself.

His fellow worker rubbed at his shirt and snickered. "Gettin' all kinds, comin' in 'ere, lately." He grumbled, waving the others down.

Niko gave them both a lopsided grin, but they had already turned away. He laughed and shrugged helplessly. Following the man's instructions, he hefted his belongings and walked carefully over to the gate where a smartly dressed official stood with his hands behind his back. He appeared bored. A bushy black beard obscured his lower face. Niko smiled broadly in greeting, noting the man's holstered weapon and stony countenance.

The man pushed his cap back and eyed the approach of the outlandishly dressed immigrant, holding up a hand as Niko came within a few feet of him.

"Hold fast there, lad." He nodded at the ship behind them. "Just arrived, have ya?" He lowered his hand, palm up. "You've your papers, I'm assuming?"

Niko kept his broad smile, his eyes bright, and nodded. "Indeed, sir." He gave a slight bow, spreading his hands out. "I am very happy to be here in your wonderful city." He straightened and dug into the side pocket of his duster for his leather wallet. "I have my papers in order and a letter of—"

"Your papers will do." The man interrupted. "And your name?"

Niko nodded again and drew forth his wallet.

"My name is Tesla, Nikola Tesla." His pine box swung around against his hip and he fumbled to right it. "One moment," he mumbled.

The official regarded the box for a moment then took a step back, placing one hand on his firearm holster, he pointed a finger at the odd looking box with his free hand. "Hold a moment, there lad. What's in that pine box?"

Niko paused. He gazed momentarily at the tense officer then looked around him. A small crowd of curious dock workers had begun to mill about, eyeing the exchange.

The officer, reading suspicion into Niko's hesitation, drew himself up and unsnapped his holster. "Gonna have to ask you to open that up, lad." He gestured to the planks at their feet. "Just set that down here and we'll have a look see, eh?"

Niko doubted this man would be able to understand, or even remotely grasp, an explanation of the contents of the box, but he kept the smile on his face and flipped his coat tails back with a slight flourish. As he knelt, he swung the box around and down onto the dock planking with a gentle motion. He bit his lip, then released the first clasp. "In here, my dear officer, is years of dedicated patience and hard work." He released the second clasp, looking up into the curious eyes of the officer as he did so. "This," he said firmly, "is a veritable labor of love." He ran his hand over the lid fondly before lifting it high. He shifted back on his heels and held out a hand.

The officer leaned in, tugging at his beard and frowning. "What in God's good name is that thing?"

TWO

Denis walked slowly through the early morning crowds on the congested streets, his hands in his pockets and limping a bit as he favored his left leg. He called it his weather forecasting leg. A childhood broken bone had left him with a sensitivity that was exacerbated by changes in weather.

Today it was extra sensitive, a deep bone ache that left him wincing with each step. He looked up and frowned. Not a cloud in the sky.

He limped around the shoeshine boys on 57th and stepped out onto the boulevard. Breathing in deeply, he tasted the cool air, heavy with the smell of coal, the earthy aroma of horse manure, and fresh garbage. He looked around, bemused and slightly distracted, only half aware of where he was going. He was having trouble shaking off the feelings that blossomed with the dawning of the day. The dreams from last night were still fresh and resonating. The edges of his vision blurred momentarily and he stopped to rub his eyes.

"Watch it!" a voice yelled down at him. The sound of horse shoes clapping the cobblestone swelled in his ears. He was jolted back to reality and stopped dead halfway across the boulevard. A wagon driver was glaring down at him from the pilot seat as he leaned back on the reins.

"'Ere now, what're you thinking?" he asked, disgust evident in his tone. "Gonna get yerself smashed!"

Denis grimaced and held up his hands placatingly.

"Sorry, friend." He apologized and hurried across the remaining distance to the opposite side of the street.

Reaching the corner he blinked and shook his head, trying to clear the fuzziness that had suddenly taken hold. Just like that he felt heavy, as if a great weight had been placed on shoulders. He leaned a hand against the gas lamp post. The smooth, cold iron was reassuring under his skin. He let out a ragged breath and gave what he hoped was a reassuring smile to the passersby watching him. They stared. Not with concern, but suspicion.

He straightened his tie and continued on, his office building was just up the next block. He limped forward and ran his hand over his shaven skull.

Denis wondered - not for the last time - what the hell was going on?

The insurance building was now just ahead. He quickened his pace as he struggled to maneuver through the crowd. He blinked. Something was wrong. A shadow had fallen over his eyes like a black veil. He almost lost his balance as his vision swam in the dimness. The faces of the people around him began to shift and change. He watched in horror as they metamorphosed before him. No longer human, the jackal faced, monstrous visages now leered back at him atop hunched humanoid bodies draped with scabrous wounds. Rotting flesh blended with torn and ripped clothing. He could almost smell the foulness. He threw a hand up to his mouth, holding back a rising gorge.

One of the horrid things reached a skeletal hand towards him.

He stumbled and cried out, flinging up tightly clenched fists in a defensive posture, ready to beat down the foul abomination before him. The thing drew back reflexively, a look of surprise on its grotesque countenance.

What was happening? His vision began to clear but his thoughts remained cloudy. He pushed the thing away and ran on, monstrous figures parting before him.

Denis breathed heavily, sweat rolling off his face, as he reached the doors to his building. He battered them open and heaved himself inside, bursting into the foyer like a bull. He stumbled over toward one of the room's squat pillars and leaned against it as he focused on maintaining his breathing.

Gotta steady this heartbeat, he thought. *Jesus, it's pounding like a damn drum.* He held his hand over his breast pocket, feeling the percussive beat of his heart and the rushing river of blood in his ears.

A throat cleared.

"Mr. Malone, are you okay, sir?" The tentative voice of concern came to him from a few feet away. Denis looked up. A round, pink-scrubbed face peeked over the edge of the desk situated at the back of the four pillared entry hall.

Voices and laughter filled the space as the door banged open and several fellow employees entered. They looked at Denis curiously, their conversation momentarily diverted. His flat stare kept them silent. They kept moving. The young boy at the desk waved at them in greeting, then turned back to Denis.

"No disrespect, you look pale - a bit sick, sir." He peered closer at him as he rose from his seat. "You want I should call a doctor?" he offered, eyes wide with concern.

Rodney's a good kid, he thought. Not like the rest of the idiots here. He blinked rapidly. Tattered shreds of darkness still clung to his peripheral vision, and that kept up the flutter of nervousness in his gut. He waved a hand and shook his head as he straightened up and stretched his neck. "That's okay, Rod, I'll be okay, just feeling a bit under the weather and foolishly decided to run the last few blocks." He managed a smile. "All good."

The young boy looked unconvinced. "If you say so, Mr. Malone."

Denis coughed and headed for the west stairwell. "Thanks Rod, oh hey-" He turned back. "How's your mum these days?"

"Much better, Sir. Thanks." He replied gratefully, his smile wide. "That doctor you told me about fixed her up good!"

Denis nodded. "Good, good. I'm glad of that." He walked on. "Keep me posted, lad," he said over his shoulder before the stairwell door closed. Denis sagged, let out a ragged breath, and slowly lowered himself down onto the bottom step. The slow, measured tread of shoes echoed hollowly in the stairwell.

"Feeling your age, old boy?" A voice tinged with amusement called out to him. Denis didn't need to turn around to know who had spoken. The footsteps gave him away. Firm heel click then forward toe tap on the marble stone - Hawthorne's confident tread.

He kept his head in his hands. "Somehow I don't think forty one years old is actually feeling my age, you jackass." He shook his head. "I'm only two months older than you," he added.

Hawthorne laughed loudly and leaned over to clap Denis on the shoulder before moving toward the door. "Doesn't matter when you look like you do right now." He tugged on the handle and looked down at his friend. "I thought I'd stop by for a morning visit but I need to run. See you at lunch. You can regale me with your no doubt sordid tale over food, you old bastard." He opened the door. "Your turn to pay the check." He laughed again.

Denis finally looked up and scowled at the man's suited retreat. The echo of his laughter bounced around the stairway then faded away to silence. Denis pulled himself to his feet muttering darkly, and stoically trudged the four flights up to his corner office.

The officer gazed down at the various pieces of metal, coils, and wires, each nestled in its own straw-lined compartment within the box. His brow furrowed in confusion, and he leveled his perplexity at this stranger while slowly shaking his head. Niko looked on, smiling triumphantly. A small crowd had gathered and was trying to catch a glimpse of what was in the box. They pushed forward, jostling those in front.

"'Ere now, steady on you lot!" the officer barked and pushed back on knees with one hand. He turned back to Niko. "Well, lad?"

Niko chewed his lip a moment then re-lit his wide smile. He reached a hand inside his coat, and with eyebrows raised, "May I?" he asked.

"Eh, what? Yes, man, get on with it!" he shouted down at Niko in exasperation.

Niko pulled out the envelope containing his letter of introduction. He smoothed it out on one knee and then offered it up to the officer. "Now, with your permission, I will show you."

Not waiting for the officer to comment either way, Niko carefully removed the foot long barrel housing from the box. He held it up for all to see as he lovingly ran his hands over the smooth, light-weight, dull grey metal.

He looked around at the circle of onlookers. "Now this, gentlemen, is the base of the resonating-coil gun." He thumbed a catch and with a click the hidden springs released a cover along the barrel.

Several "oohs" and "ahhs" filtered out from the crowded circle.

He paused a moment, squinting, and pursed his lips before continuing. "Electric power is everywhere, and contrary to what you have learned, what is persistently perpetuated even today, is that it exists in vast quantities - all around us, everywhere." With his free hand he reached into the box and withdrew a round cylindrical, carousel-like object. Several wires hung free from this piece. He held up a finger. "Knowing this, and with the proper application, we might harness this unlimited supply, no?" He snapped the cylindrical section into the open slot on top of the barrel housing.

The officer looked up from reading the letter, a slightly startled look on his face. He regarded the strange weapon in Niko's hand uncomprehendingly, then brought the letter back up to his face.

Niko flipped the barrel around with practiced ease, the movement rustling the paper in the officer's hands. "Now, certain living organisms, human and," he frowned wryly, tapping a finger on the metal,

14

"non-human, have a resonating frequency that, when identified, can be manipulated." He reached back into the box and held up the rubber wrapped stock, its worn hand grip smooth and shiny. He maneuvered this into place onto the end of the barrel. It made a satisfying loud snick. "I have made careful study of these frequencies, and have identified many, many levels." He said nothing for a few heartbeats. "This device manipulates such frequencies, see?" He pointed the weapon down toward the ground and sighted along the now completed resonating coil-gun. "Understand?" He lowered the rifle and gazed around at the group.

The officer cleared his throat.

He had finished reading and was looking at Niko with something akin to awe. "Edison, lad? That's where yer headed? To the Wizard of Menlo Park?"

Denis sat quietly at his desk, the oak chair hard against his body as he gazed out onto the morning cityscape. He leaned back, concentrating on the feeling of the firm wood against his body. He took deep breaths and focused on bringing his heart rate back to Earth. He felt that familiar craving, the smooth silkiness of bourbon would do wonders for his nerves, make him forget the images and it would be oh-so-easy, to give in. He set his jaw and regarded the clear, calm sky with suspicion and shook his head. Street sounds from below filtered up to the open windows. He had to be iron. He thought again of that horrid thing that had reached out for him. What was all that?

Those creatures, those people.

He rubbed his eyes and wondered if he was losing his mind. Snorting, he raised his eyebrows and shuddered as he barked out a laugh. "Okay, get a grip Malone. Whatever that was, it's gone and you've got work to do!"

For the next three hours he lost himself in the mindlessness of work, applying himself diligently to getting through the backlogged mountain of reports and sundry paperwork. For a small time he forgot all about the disturbing images from that morning and the odd feelings he had been suffering from for months.

A knock at his door startled him and returned him to the moment. He looked up. "It's open," he told the closed door.

A slicked back head of black hair thrust in and leaned on the half open door. "You going to work through lunch?" He looked pointedly at the clock over the west window. "No one's seen you all morning." He stopped and peered closely at Denis. "You okay? You look a bit ragged."

Denis rubbed his face, as if washing without water, then tossed down his pen. "I'm fine, Rogers. And no, I am not going to work through food." He nodded, as if to himself. "But thanks for the break."

Daniel Rogers smiled, his bushy mustache stretched wide. "You joining the boys and me, then?" He cocked his head back. "We're going over to Muldoon's. Come on."

Denis shook his head. "Got a lunch meeting with a friend," he said a bit regretfully. *Perhaps just one... No. Stop it.* Now was definitely not the time to backslide. As tempting as that might be, he needed his wits about him. Besides, he had to head over to that new client's brownstone after lunch.

Rogers shrugged. "Suit yourself. I'll see you later then." He said as he closed the door. Denis rubbed his scalp and stared at the door a moment before getting to his feet. He paused, chewing his lower lip. He studied the desk and then, with one hand, slid open the middle drawer and removed a wooden case. He ran his hands over the dark, worn wood and smiled faintly. Something told him he would be needing this. He lifted the well oiled and well kept pistol from its plush blue velvet cradle.

Raising the Dragoon up and squinting as he sighted along the lengthy barrel, he swung his arm around to the open window and pulled the trigger. The hammer fell and the metallic click sounded firm, loud, and downright comforting in the silent room. He nodded firmly as he lowered the handgun and snapped in a cylinder.

The Colt Dragoon Percussion Revolver had been issued to him during the War and had served him quite well. This particular model was a Type III and offered up a lighter weight, shorter cylinder and a vastly improved loading lever. Additionally, the Type III had an optional shoulder stock attachment complete with folding leaf sights. Denis lifted his folding shoulder stock out and slipped it into a jacket pocket.

Might need this. Never know.

Standing over the desk now, one hand tight on the Dragoon's handle, his gaze was drawn down. The lower desk drawer's brass knob was like an eye staring back at him.

"Stop that!" he growled at the desk and narrowing his own eyes, tugged the drawer open, breaking the drawer's stare. The muffled clinking of glass against wood and the sloshing of liquid whispered in his ear. It rocked a bit then stopped, nestling comfortably between a pile of paper and a few books.

Denis lowered his now sweaty gun hand and studied the bottle. The curve of the neck, the unbroken wax cork, and the gorgeous color - like maple syrup alive from within like sunlight.

This unopened bottle was his test, his reminder of the long hard road he was on. Would he pass?

Visions of rotting flesh filled his mind, and the stench of it clogged his nostrils.

Suddenly his mouth was bone dry and that old empty hole was there, waiting to be filled.

Gritting his teeth, he pointed the Dragoon at the bottle. "No, not this time. I win again." He smiled grimly and slammed the drawer shut with a satisfying bang. "That's right boyo, we Malones are fighters."

He clapped on his leather belt holster, secured the brass buckle and then tied the thigh strap. Finally, he shrugged into his light-weight quarter jacket and stepped over to the mirror. He grimaced at the dark circles under his eyes but now felt a modicum of assurance with the familiar weight of the Dragoon riding low on his hip. He settled the hat down onto his head and nodded at his reflection.

I need to get back to the ring. I'm starting to look a bit flabby. He chuckled and turned to leave, then remembered he had forgotten to remove the contract papers from his bag. He was definitely feeling off today. He pulled the sheaf of papers from the worn leather satchel, shuffled them into order, and stuffed them into the inner pocket of his jacket.

Denis locked up his office carefully and headed for the lunch meeting with his friend.

The Eye blinked. Its baleful, blue-fire rimmed gaze regarded the hooded figure before it. The orb rotated in an invisible socket to study its surroundings. It took note of everything. The drip and damp of the basement stone, the dim light cast by the ritual candles, the blood filled bowl. Most of all, it took note of its captor. Hatred and rage filled it. It drifted forward and stopped abruptly as if hitting a wall. Confining energy flared and miniature lightning bolts sparked out. The wards placed upon the summoning circle kept it confined, for now. A low, disembodied growl bubbled up and filled the room. The Eye's gaze narrowed.

The hooded figure smiled with satisfaction and watched as the dinner-plate sized Eye scrutinized the room then blinked once again as it firmly fixed its stare back on him.

He crossed his arms and nodded. "Yes. I have summoned you here. You cannot cross the place of the circle. You are here to do my bidding, and I will release you shortly. I have a task for you." He gestured toward the Eye. "A simple task, really."

The Eye watched him, unblinking, as if listening closely.

"Excellent. Now that you know your situation, I can task you."

The Eye began to growl again and strained against the circle's confining wards. Energy sparked with the contact.

The figure's laugh fell cold across the Eye's displeasure. "Do not think to disobey or cause me grief, Eye-ling, I am high in your Master's favor. Although I cannot hurt you directly, I can send you back via a very circuitous and painful route." His voice rose in command, crackling like static and cutting off any further discussion.

He began to pace back and forth in front of the circle for several moments as the Eye waited and watched. "He's here, I can feel it. I just don't know where." He muttered irritably in a low voice, as if to himself. He looked up at the Eye. It floated unconcerned.

He leveled a finger at it. "Now, here is your task."

Niko's eyes grew wide and he nodded with enthusiasm. "Yes indeed, is it not exciting?" He laughed with delight and looked about the crowded circle of people. "I am passing through your fine, magical city for a bit before I travel to Mr. Edison's laboratory in New Jersey. It is a grand opportunity and one I hope to learn much from." *And confront beings beyond even what your worst nightmare might conjure forth.*

The officer shook his head, clearly flabbergasted and out of his element. He handed the letter back to him. "Exciting indeed, young lad." He scratched his bearded jaw then gestured toward the pine box. "You need assistance packing that contraption up?"

Niko waved the offer away politely. "I will manage, good sir," he said as he began to carefully dismantle the coil gun. "But I do thank you," he added looking up at him. "I am happy to have been given the opportunity to display my invention."

The officer grunted and turned to the gathered people. "All right you lot, the show is over." He waved both hands. "Back to work and such. That's right. Move along."

Disappointed but not about to test the officer's patience, they complied, and the circle drifted apart as each man sought his own task.

Snapping the pine case shut, Niko stood and swung it onto his shoulder. He straightened his dark goggles and checked over his gear. Satisfied he smiled and offered his hand to the custom's officer. "Again, I thank you. I must prevail upon you one more time before I depart, however."

The officer took his hand and shook it heartily. "What, oh - of course lad, what'd you be needing?" he asked with raised eyebrows.

Niko tugged down on his long coat and leaned in with a smile. "Can you direct me to the Astor Library?"

THREE

Denis chewed at the side of his mouth as he sat gazing out the window, only half listening to what his friend was saying. His right hand absently toyed with the coffee spoon.

John Hawthorne was flipping through his work notebook. "Five Points has been busy, averaging a murder a night." He flipped a page. "Ah, yes, and there was that mysterious body pulled from a carriage by some unknown men and left—" He stopped, realizing he was essentially talking to himself. Leaning forward, Hawthorne cleared his throat. "I'm thinking of shaving my head and dressing like you, what do you think?"

Denis stirred. "What? Oh, yes, of course. That sounds good." He replied, his eyes still set with that thousand yard stare.

Hawthorne broke out into laughter and slapped the table. Plates and silverware jumped. Several patrons nearby stopped eating to look over. He ignored them.

"Where were you just then? Not here, that's for damn sure! I am fairly certain you were not agreeing to me shaving my head and dressing like you, old boy." He chuckled looking pointedly at Denis' rumpled suit and ragged long-coat. "You're not exactly the model of acceptable fashion, I'm afraid."

Denis blinked rapidly and turned back to his friend. "I'm sorry, John," he apologized, shaking his head. "I've been a bit distracted today." He took a swallow of lukewarm coffee and grimaced. "Seriously, what were you talking about?"

Hawthorne lifted his own mug in mock salute and sipped. "Distracted today? Ha." He smiled broadly as he set his coffee down. "You've been distracted for quite some time now." He looked at his friend, closely noting the dark circles under his eyes. "You have something you want to get off your chest?" he asked with raised eyebrows and cocked head. "And you must think I'm blind," he added.

Denis pulled his head back. "Blind? What do you mean?"

His friend nodded at the coat pulled tight over his right thigh. "You have that quick release holster strapped. I assume you're carrying your Dragoon?" he asked in a lowered voice. "That smacks of tension, my friend. Are you in trouble?" he asked lightly.

Denis glanced around the room. "It's nothing really." He shrugged and scratched at his jaw. "I'm probably being overly cautious. I've been feeling off lately and something told me to take the Dragoon with me today, that's all."

Hawthorne sat back in his chair and crossed his legs. He regarded his friend for a moment before continuing. "One of your premonitions?" He brushed at his trouser leg.

"In a matter of speaking, yeah. Been having those night terrors. More than usual." He snorted. "Probably keeping Victoria awake, but she won't tell me."

Hawthorne nodded. "She wouldn't." He agreed. "She really cares for you, old boy." He rested his cheek on a closed fist. "Now, these nightmares. Is there a theme to them?" he asked.

Denis squinted his eyes and shook his head. "Sometimes, but overall I get these images, see? Rapid flashes of things - places, people, from some other time, I think. I don't know." He fidgeted in his seat. "I get the sense I am looking down on events, like a ghost floating above." He shuddered. "And then I wake up screaming and sweating." He dropped his gaze to the table. "And that's not the strangest part…" he murmured quietly to his half eaten lunch. He shook his head. *This is too crazy, I've never told anyone this before, not even Victoria. I'm not ready. Not sure I even know it wasn't a dream despite the intense realness of what I viewed.* He turned a weary gaze back to his friend. "It's been exhausting, John."

Hawthorne watched him for a moment, then pursed his lips. "I assume you have already visited a physician?" he gestured with his notebook. "Nothing of a physical nature is consuming you?"

"No, nothing. I'm in great condition." He slapped his chest. "Well, aside from the lack of sleep, that is," he added.

His friend nodded and then his face took on a rueful, apologetic look. "I am sorry but I have to ask—"

Denis' own face turned stony. "I know what you're going to say and absolutely not, man!"

Hawthorne held up his hands in peace. "I know, I know," he shrugged. "But you see my position?" He straightened, leaning across the table and tapped a forefinger on the wood. "I'm your friend, I'm concerned, and if you ever need help—" He looked at his friend.

Denis waved that away, his anger melted but annoyance still lingered. "I understand but I'm fine." He waved his hand wildly. "Gods, you and Victoria are going to drive me insane," he hissed.

Hawthorne smiled tolerantly, willing to let the matter drop, then looked around for the serving woman. "I'll see to the coffee, old boy, in the meantime settle down."

Denis drained the last drops of cold coffee and let his annoyance fall away. He was determined to enjoy the rest of his lunch visit before making his way to the house of his new client. He consulted his pocket watch. It was almost one o'clock. He had some time left, but not much.

"Look, Hawthorne—" he started to say, then stopped as a figure outside the window caught his eye, making him pause. A wave of vertigo slapped him and he clutched at the table top as a staccato flash of white light obscured his vision for a split second. "What the hell—" he mumbled.

In the background he could hear Hawthorne talking to a serving woman, the voices muffled and far away sounding. His fingers dug into the scarred wood. He looked out the window again. His vision tunneled and he blinked trying to scatter the darkness from his peripheral vision. The shallow ground fell away. The world spun and threatened to fling him off.

Not again!

Pausing outside the window was a young man, perhaps in his late twenties, looking like he didn't belong there on the streets of New York City. Denis shook his head, marveling at both the outlandish garb and the stranger's aura of familiarity.

Hawthorne's voice brought him back to Earth.

Denis blinked, giving him a vacant look.

Hawthorne pocketed his notebook then consulted his own watch. "Don't you have an appointment?" he said, looking at Denis with one raised eyebrow. "Go. I'll take care of this." He waved his hand at the table.

"Thanks, John." He stood up again, this time with more finesse and grabbed his hat. "Looks like I'm grabbing a cab."

His friend nodded. "Now you have two meals to pay for next round."

Denis crammed his hat on his head and squared it off neatly and nodded. "I'll see you later then."

He stepped out and joined the stream of people, a subdued feeling of dread settling around his chest. He shook himself then turned his attention to finding a free cab.

Time to go back to work.

Niko stopped walking and paused to get his bearings. He stepped closer to the window to avoid the passing people and pulled out the little hand drawn map and directions that the officer was kind enough to provide for him. The parchment crinkled in his hand.

He held it up, scanning the neat handwriting and the crude, yet effective little map, then smiled. *Very accurate,* he thought approvingly. He twisted and turned to gaze across the street. *There.* He was close and needed to head in that direction. But first - he pocketed the map and thrust back his coat - he wanted to check his aural reader.

The people of New York City flowed by him, oblivious.

Niko pushed back the coat flap and unclipped the aural reader, letting the rifle bump against his thigh as his coat closed. It was a comforting weight and helped to keep him grounded. He toggled a black button, chirping the unit into life. Small lights awoke, declaring their ready state.

For a brief moment his thoughts flashed back to his brother, Dane. He grimaced thinking that it was somehow wrong to feel comforted by the presence of a weapon. He wondered, not for the last time, what his brother would think of all of this. He smiled, then again, if it was not for the untimely death of his brother, his own presence would not be needed here now.

Why me? That question bounced around his head with a familiar motion and then echoed back to him was the same response.

Because there is no one else.

One, Two, Three. He moved the aural reader in a fanning motion, slowly from left to right across the space in front of him. Several people stared. He ignored them and watched the receptors rise more than halfway. It was locking onto the trail. He pointed the device across the street in the direction the map indicated. The lights chirped red.

He switched it off and returned the unit to his belt, turning toward the window slightly, and felt someone watching him. He raised his head sharply and stepped closer to the glass.

A shaven headed man in a gray suit sat with another. His chair was turned towards the window. Their eyes locked. Niko felt the raw power of recognition jolt him. His eyes widened slightly. Could it be? This stranger was awash in blue-white fire, announcing his own latent ability. The man shot to his feet, tipping his chair back. No time to stop. Pity. Niko had come across precious few with the gift. No matter, he needed to move.

Another time.

Niko smiled crookedly at the man, winked and disappeared into the crowd.

Denis stalked and staggered out into the street, searching this way and that for a carriage, trying to figure out just how the day managed to slip from his control. He tasted the bile on the back of his throat and suddenly wanted to punch something.

He hailed an approaching cab, stepping back as it settled to a stop in front of him. Denis sniffed. All that time in the saddle riding with the Cavalry yet he remained steadfast in his dislike of the fragrance of horse. The driver pulled the brake and leaned over tipping his hat. Denis cleared his throat and pulled himself into seat.

"I need to get to this address, quickly." He directed, handing the man a card.

The cabbie glanced briefly at it then nodded as he released the brake. "Will do, captain," he replied, flicking his whip lightly. The cab jerked into motion and clattered along the cobblestone, moving briskly into the flow of traffic and down the boulevard.

Denis settled in and rested his hand on the concealed Dragoon, wondering what the hell the day was going to throw at him next.

Niko strode purposefully up the marble steps of the Astor Library, his eyes darting over the German, Rundbogenstil style architecture. He pulled a deep breath and counted the shallow steps one by one as he moved over them.

Three, four, five. He moved quickly while mentally reviewing what he already knew of the *Liber de Voltus*. Over 400 years old, this archaic tome was penned by an old monk around 1469 in Italy. His many years of searching and research had led him here. Of course, there was a chance it was not here. A book that old, you never knew. He shuddered inwardly and tried not to think of that as he thrust open the massive wooden door and stepped inside the cool, small interior rotunda.

He squinted as his eyes adjusted to the dimness. It was quiet and the scent of book ink and old parchment was a heavy touch on his senses.

Breathing in the Library's heady perfume, Niko entered into the inner chamber through the smaller doors. Massive shelving lined and crowded the stone walls. Niko smiled broadly at the sheer weight of information and knowledge contained in one building.

"May I help you, sir?" a soft, but strong voice questioned.

He turned toward the sound, his eyebrows raised. A short, slender young woman with shoulder length auburn hair and sharp, bright green eyes gazed curiously up at him. Her face had a classic beauty that tugged at his heart. It was a face sculpted by winds not of this City. She balanced a small armful of leather bound books in the crook of her arm.

She looked him up and down, taking in his goggles, three piece suit, and long travel-worn and stained coat.

He grinned at her and executed a small bow. "Yes, indeed, Ms.—?"

"My name's Hazel," she said. "Hazel Carter." She shifted her books and held out her hand.

"Ah, yes, forgive me." He took her hand and shook it firmly. "My name is Tesla, Nikola Tesla, but please, call me Niko."

Hazel smiled warmly. "Niko," she repeated, letting his name roll off her tongue. "I like that," she added then looked pointedly at his clothing. "You don't look like you're from around here."

He looked down at himself and chuckled softly. "Indeed, no Ms. Carter. I am just arrived here from overseas."

She nodded with pleasure. "Please, call me Hazel." She pointed to the box slung over his shoulder. "Would you like to put that down?"

He shifted the pine box and gave her a lop-sided grin. "I will be okay carrying this, Hazel, thank you." He paused to adjust the leather strap then continued. "I was born in Serbia. I have been traveling around for some time." His eyes searched the quiet library for a moment, then turned back to her. "My quest has led me here to this island city."

"Quest, is it?" she responded, cocking her hip. "That is both impressive and mysterious, Niko." Her eyes narrowed. "And now you are here," she added shrewdly.

He nodded and leaned closer, grabbing her free hand. She caught her breath, startled, but didn't pull away. She looked up at him, caught in his gaze. His eyes were so bright, so alive. She saw sadness and pain along with something else she could not define or put words to. Her eyes softened. This man has known loss.

She took a small step forward, relaxing her stance. Her books fell to the floor scattering and echoing the room. She jumped but maintained their handhold.

Niko gazed at her steadily, his dark eyes holding her captive in that moment.

"Yes! And now, please," he squeezed her hand gently and drew her close. "Your rare book collection, take me there."

"Okay," she whispered softly, wondering at the ease at which she readily agreed to this strange man.

FOUR

The Eye-ling sped through the summer sky, crackling and streaming with living energy. It thrust the warm air aside, all but invisible to the human senses. Flocks of birds squawked with annoyance as it burst through their tidy flight formations.

Unconcerned with the primitive winged creatures, it rocketed onward. Compelled to complete its task, the eye concentrated on the faint psychic trail the human sorcerer had impressed upon it.

With a flash, energy ignited, and the Eye stopped abruptly, as if hitting a stone wall. It hovered and drifted slightly in the winds aloft as its gaze followed the now visible line, glowing like a silver cord, down to the city below.

It expanded momentarily as if puffing up in triumph and it locked in on this vibration, once more speeding off, running the silver cord like a track.

The cooler air sent a shiver along Niko's spine and he was grateful to be wearing his coat. Hazel seemed unaffected by the change in temperature as they descended the wooden staircase. He followed her down, the oil lamp she carried surrounding her in a halo of soft golden light.

"It's just down here," she said over her shoulder. "The rare book room is back along the North Wall in the section where we keep our remainders." He nodded although she could not see him. He continued his count of each step in time with the firm click her heels made on the old wood.

She stopped when she reached the bottom and turned to him. "Our rare book room is fairly large. Do you know what your book looks like?"

He paused on the last step, his coat brushing her leg. He nodded once peering into the shadows. "The *Liber de Voltus* is a smallish, leather bound book, perhaps a half-inch deep." He held up his thumb and forefinger. "The cover face is stamped with a coin sized bluish metallic rune." He looked at her and shot her his lop-sided smile. "But, I don't need to see it to find it," he added.

Her eyebrows danced. "Okay, Niko, that sounds crazy to me." She retracted her head slightly. "And we really don't know each other that well for you to make odd pronouncements like that." She eyed his strange outfit, taking in the pine box slung across his shoulder and the dark goggles pushed high upon his forehead. His thick hair stuck out in disarray.

"True enough, but it is also true that the book gives off an aura." He shook his head. "I do not expect you to believe. However, I can sense this energy, these auras. Ever since I was a small boy I could do so."

Hazel looked at him, not sure what to think of that. She stayed silent.

He smiled patiently. "It is better that I show you," he pointed into the darkness.

"Over here," Hazel spoke in a hushed tone better served for churches and not empty basement libraries as she moved toward a heavy, iron bound oak door. "Here, hold this," she said, handing him the lamp. "This lock can be difficult."

Niko stopped and looked at her with amusement. "Why are we whispering?" he asked, taking the lamp from her. "There is no one here."

"What?" She stood at the door, busying herself with the lock. "Oh, I don't know." She shrugged but then continued in a more normal tone. "Libraries bring it out in me, I suppose, and honestly—" she twisted her head to look around. "This place feels holy." The golden lamplight caught her wide green eyes, reflecting back the passion in her voice. "Don't you feel it?"

He nodded at her approvingly. "I do indeed," he responded in a quieter voice.

She laughed, a strong, clear sound that warmed Niko. For a quick moment he wished he was here just for the sake of the knowledge itself and not working against the damn clock to stop an evil from spreading.

There was a sharp click. "There." Hazel pushed open the old door sending years of dust dancing and swirling up into the musty air.

Holding the lamp high, Niko stepped forward, the light illuminating a forty by forty foot room lined with heavy, floor to ceiling bookcases. Two large tables occupied the center of the room, books everywhere. The shelves were packed tightly and every available space on the tables was covered with book stacks of varying heights. Here and there on the floor, book piles rose like hills along the stone floor.

Hazel stood next to him and waved her hand across the room. "See? It's not too terribly disorganized, but there are a lot of books here." She looked around, frowning. "I do need to get in here and catalog," she mumbled critically.

Niko nodded but said nothing as he held the lamp out to her. "If you please? I shall need both hands free to do this." He held up his free hand and wiggled his fingers.

Hazel took the lamp back from him. She regarded him silently, eyes bright, and she found herself holding her breath. She exhaled and shivered. Despite the strangeness of it all, she could not help but feel excitement. *What was he going to do? Cast a spell? Pull a wand out and wave it around?*

"It's over here," he said pointing to the bookcase to the right as he strode toward it.

"What?" Her shoulders sagged. "That's it?"

Niko looked over to her, his features puzzled. "What were you expecting?"

She set the lamp down on the corner of the table, the only open space free of books. "Oh, I don't know, something more." She made a flourish with her hand. "You didn't do anything!"

"Oh, you mean perhaps, a theatrical spell of some sort? 'Eye of newt' and such?"

"Yes!"

He smiled. "I am sorry, my dear Hazel, it does not work that way." He turned back to the bookcase and quickly scanned the shelves. He knelt down, holding his left hand out, palm facing the book spines. "At least, not with me."

Curious, Hazel bent down quietly next to him.

Breathing slowly, deliberately and starting from the leftmost book, Niko passed his hand slowly to the right.

The faintest of tingles blossomed along his fingertips.

There!

Niko swiveled his head to look at Hazel. He winked, and reached in, almost at the middle point of the shelf, and drew forth a slender, leather bound volume.

Silently, he held up the book, displaying for her the runic symbol on the cover.

With wide eyes, Hazel leaned into him, shivering. "You found it, just like that," she said, with hushed voice and breath steaming in the cold air.

Wait. Cold air? Niko's eyes widened as he pushed out a breath. They both watched it plume white in the suddenly frigid air of the rare book room. There was now a baleful silence in the room and the book-lined walls felt sinister.

Hazel looked at him, startled and with a hint of fear in her voice. "What's wrong?" she asked in a low voice, her eyes darting around the room. "Why is it so cold all of a sudden?" she asked, rubbing her arms to warm them.

"Something is coming, if not already here." He looked around the room then shrugged the pine box off his shoulder. It swung around onto the floor next to them. "Here, please hold this," he said handing her the book.

Hazel reached for the slim book, her face an excited mask of curiosity. "What is in there?" she asked pointing at the box. "Hopefully something to warm us up?"

He flashed her a quick smile and thumbed the two latches, the click of their release loud in the cold air.

"Oh wow."

Niko held the base stock by the rubber grip and began to assemble the Resonating Coil Gun pieces. "Hazel, I need you to remain calm, no matter what happens next." Click. "Can I count on you to do that for me?" He swung the carousel coil housing and slammed it home, clicking it into place. "I won't let anything harm you," he added bringing the now assembled rifle up in front of a wide-eyed Hazel.

She looked at him. *He looks so grim but focused. The pain in his eyes is gone. This is related somehow.* She silently nodded - and almost too overwhelmed to speak - watched him attach a red wire from the heavy belt at his waist to the shoulder stock end of the gun.

Out in the main room, there was a flash of bright blue light and a sharp retort as if someone had snapped a piece of wood in half. The sound of it echoed in the smaller room. Hazel jumped, falling back onto her ass as Niko swiveled his feet toward the door.

There was a faint vibration in the air, a hum as if heard from a distance, far away but growing louder.

Niko stood in one fluid motion, flipping back his open coat like a gunslinger. With one hand he trained his weapon on the open doorway as he toggled the switch on his belt. A small answering hum filled the space around him as the power within the coil flared to life.

The little turbine within the round housing began to spin.

The vibrating hum from outside the door intensified. Blue light illuminated the darkness and filled the space outside. Energy crackled and shadows fled.

Just like that fateful night, twenty years ago. That same power. That same elemental energy.

To her credit, Hazel did not scream in terror, but she gasped as the disembodied Eye now stared at them around the door frame.

Niko grunted and lowered the gun. *Just an Eye-ling.* He felt movement at his side. He looked down to see Hazel hiding behind him and smiled reassuringly.

She clutched at him. "What is that?" She hissed in a strained whisper. "I mean, it's an eye, obviously, but -" She leaned in closer. "It's just an eye, floating there."

"Yes indeed, but so much more than that." He pulled the rifle up and turned back to address the creature. "Is that not correct?" he said with his voice raised.

The Eye-ling nudged itself around the door jam, filling the doorway with blue-white light. Tiny arcs of static electricity continually fell from it. The pupil widened slightly as it rotated to take in the small room. Silently satisfied it fixed its gaze back upon Niko.

A voice, sounding tinny, hollow, and far away emanated from the creature. "I am curious how you managed to track me so quickly." The voice grunted with annoyance. "You're far beyond making me angry," the voice stated matter-of-factly as the pupil became a slit. "Every damn time, interrupting my work, causing me delays." The Eye pulsed and seemed to pull in a breath as it shrank then grew larger, filling the doorway more completely. "I can keep you here now until I am finished the ritual." A soft chuckle filled the cold air. "The stars are right, once again, as you no doubt know already." The eye bobbed as if nodding. "And that gun is quite useless. Bullets will not harm this construct. You forget yourself, boy."

Niko said nothing.

Hazel squeezed his arm. "That thing likes to talk, doesn't it?" she observed. "Where is the voice coming from?"

"The voice is a projection. The eye itself is a magical construct, typically conjured to run errands and serve as a second," he said, waving his free hand at the Eye. Additionally, the conjurer can see what the Eye sees. Quite clever and convenient, really, despite the source."

The Eye somehow managed to look indignant. "Humph! I am floating right here, you know," the voice said. "No need to be insulting."

Niko released a slow breath then, holding up a finger at the Eye, and checked the power meter on his belt. Satisfied, he lowered his dark goggles. "Hazel, please close your eyes," he told her softly, keeping his darkened gaze on the Eye.

"You are quite correct," he told the voice. Niko turned a small knob next to the grip. He made a quick mental calculation and swiftly dialed in the setting. "Bullets are no use. However," he raised the rifle and placed his free hand on the rubber grip on the barrel. "This weapon does not utilize bullets," he said as he gave the Eye a lopsided smirk. Looking back at Hazel, he winked, then pulled the trigger on the Coil Gun.

The miniature turbine housed in the round carousel had been patiently spinning and generating energy, waiting for release. Miniature bursts of lightning flared and hissed forth like an angry slew of snakes.

The stored energy was a tidal wave, a ripping tornado of pure elemental force. Mother Nature herself would be hard pressed to mimic this. Blue-white fire arced and streamed out from the rifle, ripping the air apart and slamming into the Eye like a hammer.

There was a staccato crackle as books took flight and were imprisoned within the whipping vortex of air. Loose papers flamed brilliantly then fluttered to ash.

Niko gritted his teeth and dug his feet in, hunkering low, his left leg rooted firm. *I think I've miscalculated.* Sweat began to run and sting his eyes but he dared not reach up to clear them. Blinking rapidly, he tightened his grip, knuckles standing out white against the blood red tinge of his shaking hands.

And gloves would be a good idea, too. His jaw was aching and his taut muscles were flooding with pain. He wasn't sure how long he could hold this nor how long the battery pack would last.

The voice from the Eye shrieked in agony, an echoing counterpoint to his own mad, primal bellow. The ground trembled and groaned in protest, books toppled off the shelves, and pyramid piles of old books spilled over onto the floor.

Hazel, her eyes clamped tightly shut, screamed and clapped her hands over her ears.

Denis was only half listening.

"'Ere, now, captain." The cabbie pointed with his free hand, the other hand expertly grasping the reins. "Look at this crowd."

"What, where?" Lost in thought, Denis roused himself, swiveling his head as he sat up. He frowned. "What about them?" he said. He noticed nothing amiss. It was just a normal crowded New York street. *Thankfully,* he thought.

The cabbie clicked his tongue and maneuvered around a stalled ice truck. He made a rude gesture to the driver. "Right-o, then. You don't see?" he asked over his shoulder, shaking his head. "There's too many of them, of us," he stated firmly, answering his own question. He spat over the side. "These 'ere tenements and whatnot, we're getting packed in like rats!"

Denis couldn't argue with that. "That's true," he growled in agreement. "This island isn't what it used to be," he snorted. "Progress, my arse - hey watch out!"

Not missing a beat, the cabbie swerved deftly around the work gang. "Pfaa! Progress. Dirty word, that." He grumbled to himself as he set them back on course.

They trundled onward for some time, the cabbie now silent as he gave himself over to driving, lost in his own thoughts of overpopulation and greener pastures.

The cabbie cleared his throat. "Almost there, captain."

Denis opened his eyes and looked around. They were getting close to the neighborhood now. The large crowds and stench gave way to quiet, tree lined streets. The noise of the city was a faint buzz behind them. Denis' stomach felt hollow. His palms began to sweat.

Shite, what now?

"What was that address there?" the cabbie asked as they turned onto the street.

Denis repeated the address again.

"Right. End of the block it seems, captain." He gazed about and around. "This here street is nice enough, but - feels off," he added softly. "Too quiet."

Denis leaned forward and looked at him sharply. "You feel it too?" he hissed.

The cabbie shrugged. "Odd, right?" he shook the reins, urging his mare forward. "Hup, now."

They rattled along the silent street.

"Where the hell is everyone?" Denis demanded. He pulled out his watch. "It's almost one o'clock."

They were halfway down the city block when the horse pulled back, neighing wildly. The cab jerked to a stop, sending both driver and passenger lurching forward.

Denis reached for his gun. The cabbie clutched the reins.

"'Ere, now Mildred, what's the problem with ya? There's no one about for you to take on like this," the driver called out, trying to soothe his frightened mare.

Mildred snorted and reared back slightly. She chuffed and shook her head, eyes rolling nervously.

Denis scanned the streets behind them. Clearly, something nearby was wrong. He could feel it and apparently so could Mildred.

"What is that?" The cabbie's hat was tilted back as he was gazing up the street, his head raised, and quavering finger pointing.

Denis turned, following his gaze. His eyes widened and he muttered "Oh, shite" from his clenched jaw. The fingers of his right hand twitched to unleash the Dragoon from the confining hold of the leather holster. He grimaced. *Not that it would do much good.* He balled a fist and took in the scene before him.

The air was shimmering as if with heat above the last house on the corner, the castle-looking brownstone. The flame-like waves were like dark, oily smoke, tinged with red from within as if from hot coals. Tendrils of the flame leaped with force, almost as if angry. He squinted, not sure if he could trust his eyes. *Was that? Yes.* It seemed as if shapes, horribly grotesque and twisted figures, were writhing inside that smoke! The whole horrid mass gave him a sense of vertigo and he grasped the side of the carriage. It seemed to Denis' eyes as if the black flames were one continuous birth and death of shadowy figures. One would rise, a half formed black skull leaping forth with a silent scream. It would stretch, reaching out with grasping talon-like claws but break apart as the next shadow emerged with intensity to take its place.

He watched, drawn to the chaos, fascinated and repulsed. He could feel his grip on reality slipping downward, spiraling away into madness.

He tore his eyes away, shuddering inwardly as he focused on his breathing. "So this is how it's going to be," he said to himself with a resigned voice. Something about this tugged him. The unsettled tension he'd felt in the morning had slowly and insistently grown as the day wore on. It was leading up to this, to here. He could not explain it. He only knew he was needed in some fashion.

"You said it, captain!" The cabbie, eyes now averted from the mess, jumped down from his perch to calm his horse. He whispered calming words to Mildred while keeping a firm grip on her reigns.

Denis one handed the release on his holster, freeing the Dragoon and shook his head. "I have no idea what in God's name that is, it's nothing I've ever seen before." He replied answering the cabbie's earlier question.

"That's not the half of it, captain." He nodded up the street. "That there devil work is surroundin' your house." He pointed. "That be the house number there." He patted his horse's flank reassuringly. "Mildred and I'll wait fer you here, I'm thinkin'."

Of course, that would have to be the house now, wouldn't it, And here I was, wondering what was in store for me next. Jesus, they don't pay me enough for this.

FIVE

Niko patted out the last of the flaming paper and heaved a sigh of relief. "That's the last of it." He sniffed and wrinkled his nose. He was reminded of the time one winter evening when his father had fallen asleep reading before the fireplace. A book had slipped from slack fingers to drop upon the hearth. The smell of the singed paper was sharp in his nose and the image of his father scrambling to extinguish the flame remained vivid even today.

"Are you sure you are all right?" he asked, walking toward her.

Hazel had picked herself up off the floor the moment the chaos ended, the sound of her own scream echoing in her head as she ran around the room putting out the resulting small fires. She was now kneeling by the door gathering rogue papers and being careful to avoid the clear ooze, all that was left of the floating Eye.

She looked over at him with wide eyes and slowly shook her head. "What was that thing?" she straightened, smoothing her skirt as she walked up to him.

He echoed her steady gaze but said nothing.

"Please, tell me, what's going on, Niko?" She moved closer to him, and gently laid the back of her palm along his soot-stained cheek. "Who are you?" she asked softly. She wanted to know this strange, gentle man. She couldn't explain it, yet it felt right to her. They say that the eyes are the windows to the soul. Niko's were both unfathomable and so telling, all at the same time. She was hooked, trapped albeit willingly, and if only she could catch just a small glimpse, a little piece, of what was raging inside him now. She stared, drawn into those deep wells and felt herself sinking. She didn't want to move. Didn't want to take her fingers away from his beautiful, pale face.

Niko held her eyes with a cool determination. He didn't pull away from her touch, but her fingers were hot against his face and he felt a stirring in his blood. He felt his heart quicken and his lips formed a small, rueful smile.

Perhaps in another life. He could feel it on his face. An almost imperceptible anguish, a tightening around his eyes and clenching of his jaw. Inexplicably, he couldn't hide his sadness from her. He felt grateful for the concern he saw flickering in her large green eyes. His heart swelled and thawed just a bit then and for the first time in quite a while Niko felt a great regret and sorrow in his decision to walk this path.

We must all follow our own paths. Design our own lives. And mine? Always alone. For now.

His fingers closed over hers for a moment squeezing softly before removing her hand. How could he let harm come to her, this amazing light that was called Hazel?

I cannot.

Red faced, she smoothed back a curtain of hair with one hand and lowered her head in embarrassment.

Placing a gentle hand upon each side of her face, Niko drew her forward and lightly pressed his lips to her forehead. He pulled in a breath, enjoying for a moment the fleeting ghost of her scent amidst the mix of burnt-paper and woodsmoke smells.

He straightened and steeled himself for the next move. "I must leave, Hazel. Time passes swiftly and the menace is still out there." He lifted her chin with his finger. "I have no doubt we shall meet again." He reached into his pocket. "And for now, I need to borrow this." He held up the ancient tome, the carven metal rune glinting with inner light.

Hazel laughed and the book once again disappeared into his pocket.

Feeling the insistent pull of the clock, he turned quickly, and with few swift strides, lifted his weapon from the center table. He glanced about the room, then checked the energy levels. Satisfied, he hooked the butt onto the inside holster sewn cleverly into his long coat. The pine box would not do now. Speed was needed. He consulted his pocket watch. He had to move quickly now, the aura left by the passing of the Eye-ling could still be followed. He smiled grimly and turned back to Hazel.

Hazel returned his smile. "Now I know you're returning." She pointed to the book. "You have to bring that back to me and pick up your pine box too." Somehow, she knew his intent was true. She would see him again, book or no book. Of that she was certain.

"Indeed." He waved an arm at the disheveled room. "And this room needs some work. I confess, my weapon was a bit, ah, enthusiastic. You may need my assistance in setting back in order." He chuckled and turned to go. "Until we meet again, Hazel." He gave her a small bow and his lopsided smile.

She blinked, and he was gone.

The Eye-ling was no more. The psychic link was destroyed.

The cult leader winced in pain. He had not expected the boy to unleash such raw electrical power from a mundane device such as that apparatus. He blinked rapidly and massaged his temples. The throbbing was subsiding quickly, but a sharp, white-hot dot of pain remained behind his left eye. He had to admit, it was a clever contraption and he could not help but admire the boy. He had come a long way since that day, twenty years ago.

He coughed. Not sure what was burning more, his eye, or his ego, he staggered to his feet and called out loudly for his servant.

"Maxwell!" he bellowed, his voice reverberating with power.

Seconds later the latch on the door to the basement clicked and quick footsteps announced the view of a tall, thin man dressed in black.

"Yes sir?" Maxwell paused in the smoky air to regard his Master. "Are you well?" He descended to the bottom step. "I thought I heard something not long ago but was reluctant to disturb you." He peered sharply and gestured at the altar.

The Master adjusted and dusted his robes as he cleared his throat. "Indeed, yes, I am fine." He waved a dismissive hand. "Merely a small annoyance and minor setback." He strode back to the altar and righted fallen candlesticks.

"Bring me the girl," he growled.

Out on the street, Denis looked back over his shoulder to where the horse and carriage waited. He could see the driver, one hand gripping tight on the reins and the other stroking Mildred's neck. He was saying something to her, no doubt in an attempt to soothe her nerves.

Denis turned his attention back to the empty street ahead and strode with cautious intent. His eyes roamed the buildings on both sides of the street for any sign of life or movement.

Nothing. Downright wrong. The fingers of one hand nervously drummed a light staccato beat on the handle of the Dragoon as he made progress towards the corner brownstone. His shoulders were tight. He tried to shrug the tension loose as he walked. He half expected something to materialize out of thin air and ambush him. Laughing to himself, he cast another nervous look behind him. The cabbie, watching him, waved in encouragement.

Denis shook his head. At least Mildred looked more calm.

The closer he approached, the more detailed the strange phenomenon emanating from the building became. He squinted as he walked closer. They were definitely humanoid shapes, although nothing suggesting a human. Denis wasn't a religious person by far, but he found himself muttering The Lord's Prayer. He grimaced, trying to focus. His booted footsteps seemed unnaturally loud in the still air.

The air was heavy, more so than anything that nature herself could manifest, and he could feel it seeping into his bones. It was a low hum, a faint vibration emanating from within.

His stomach knotted as he felt the strength of the house deepen as he got closer. The swirling mass of smoky shapes were now speeding up. Shadowy taloned claws reached for him as he approached.

Denis stopped and paused to watch. The stone stairs were before him. He tilted his head up the dozen or so steps and checked the heavy oak door. The shadowy mass surrounding the building did not obscure the stairs or the door. He frowned and swallowed a rising lump in his throat. His eyes darted about the building and he tried to quell a blossoming disquiet in his stomach. Of all that he had seen these past twenty years, this chaos here made him feel like a raw recruit, fresh from the ranks and green. He closed his eyes briefly and breathed in.

Hold fast Denis, lad, he mouthed silently. He opened his eyes again. The door was before him. This was the only way in. He watched the shadow shapes reaching and flowing. He shook his head wondering why he was here. He looked back in the direction of the carriage. There was no way in hell he was going to touch the shadows to test one of those ground floor windows. Of course, he did have a legitimate reason for being here after all, so knocking on the front door was not all that unreasonable. He wondered again what this particular house contained that was in need of insurance. Keeping one eye on the house, he consulted his watch. He smiled in grim amusement.

Time to go to work.

Niko ran though the library, his coat streaming behind him. His rifle bounced against his thigh and one hand held up his aural compass before him. The odds were slim but he was hoping against all hope that he would be able to pick up the trail.

He thrust open the library doors into the warm June sunlight, scattering pigeons as he searched the skies frantically.

Nothing yet.

He checked the compass, holding it at arm's length and swinging it slowly in a wide arc from left to right across his chest.

The steady, faint pinging, which usually indicated normal levels, grew perceptibly louder and the red light brightened noticeably with the tell-tale sign of residual energy.

Yes! He looked up and over at the direction he needed to follow.

Niko strode off confidently in the direction of the river front.

Many people watched in amazement at the strangely clad young man striding through the city streets waving some mechanical contraption back and forth. They took one look at his grim face, fever bright eyes, and parted to let him pass. Others gave him only cursory inspection before turning back to their own affairs, content in their own troubles.

He didn't get too far.

There was a faint rumbling as if from far off thunder. The sky darkened, hiding the sun behind roiling black clouds.

People stopped to look up and point. A chill wind began to blow up the street bringing with it a scent of rot and decay.

From off in the distance, dogs barked and howled.

The ping of the aural compass became one long drawn out sound and the red indicator light remained on.

But which way to go now? Niko searched, frustrated and momentarily at a loss.

Which way?

As if in answer, the ominous grumble of thunder grew louder and seemed to Niko to emanate from the West where the sky seemed even darker.

"Looks like we're in for a summer thunderstorm," a voice at his side said knowingly.

Niko blinked and turned. A grizzled old man stood staring at the sky. He nodded and smiled toothily.

Niko smiled back and was about to respond when he was stopped short by a voice that thundered down from the sky. It boomed and echoed above their heads with eldritch words that could only come from something beyond mortal ken. Something as ancient as the stars.

DEES MEES JARSCHET BOEN MOESEF LOUVEMA ENTIMAUS!

The ground trembled and heaved as if the very Earth herself were repulsed from the words pounding down from the aether. People screamed and ran, seeking shelter from the chaos.

Niko grabbed the old man's arm, catching him as he stumbled. "What devilry is this, lad?" he shouted into Niko's face. "What's happening?" Fingers dug into his arm. "Are the hounds of hell come at last?" His breath reeked faintly of grain alcohol.

Niko steadied the man and thrust his own coat back. "It's not a thunderstorm, good Sir." He pocketed his compass. "Nor are they hounds." He smiled wryly and nodded. "But hell is indeed close." He released the buckle and drew his rifle from its inner holster. He leaned in and brought his face close to the old man's. "You need to take shelter," he said, "and wait for the sun to reappear."

The old man stood frozen with wide, frightened eyes and nodded silently.

Niko broke into a reassuring smile and patted the man's shoulder. "All will be well." He plugged his rifle into the battery pack and flicked on the power switch. The machine hummed comfortingly to life. The man looked from the rifle and back to Niko, almost too stunned to speak.

"Wha-what is that?" he asked, finding his voice and pointing to Niko's weapon. "Never seen a rifle like that!"

"And nor will you again." Niko replied then turned to leave. "I have to get to work."

The old man just shook his head.

Niko ran toward that dark tempest.

Despite the chaotic swirling mass covering the house, all was silence. No sound, no sun, not a hint of air movement at all. Denis blinked, stifled an unbidden tiredness, and fought off a serious yawn. The thickness of the atmosphere caused his eyelids to drop low. His head felt like it was wrapped in cotton.

Moving slowly, and as steady as he could muster, he placed one booted foot upon the lower step. Holding a breath, he winced and braced himself for the attack he was certain was about to assail him.

Nothing.

The shadow's shapes quickened their dance and rolled toward him but seemed, mercifully, unable to reach him.

He stared intently at the black mass as the shapes metamorphosed from one hellish figure into another. He took another step up, then drew a sharp breath. *There! No, it couldn't be. Could it?* He leaned in, peering closer, trying to ascertain the validity of what he was seeing. He shook his head vigorously as if to clear away the familiar images now forming there and blinked. There it was again. The shape, the face, before him now was that of-

"No!" He cried out, throwing up his free hand. Heart-wrenching, unbidden images of the battle on Cavalry Field flooded his vision.

He stumbled back a pace and almost fell. Something hissed in his ear and he closed his eyes and bowed his head. The Lord's Prayer flitted through his loose grip on sanity and bounced around those images, shattering and dispelling them like so many toy soldiers.

He swallowed, righting himself, and gripped the Dragoon's handle. He attempted to conjure up saliva from a desert-dry mouth.

His breath quickened as he approached the front door. He could feel the icy sinews of fear winding around his heart. If ever there was a desire for a drink, it was now.

A clenched hand hovered inches above the smooth wood as he paused to regard once again the strange shadows flowed outward, rising and falling like waves across the facade of the house. The images of the people on the street came back to him in a flood. They were the same creatures. He shuddered inwardly, his stomach knotting. Considering what was occurring, knocking on the front door seemed moronic and futile.

Something unwholesome was happening, foregoing the usual etiquette was warranted.

Denis tried the door latch.

Locked.

He tensed, looking about once more. Seeing no one, he took a deep breath, and sharply kicked the door just below the latch.

The latch mechanism shattered with a tremendous crack, blasting the door open as wood splinters fluttered like snow against the darkness of a silent foyer. Denis pulled the Dragoon free and sidestepped up to the ruin of the door frame, weapon held high and ready. He checked the outside of the building one final time.

The shadow creatures rose and fell, swirling, ignoring him.

He grunted, nodded satisfactorily to himself, then stepped up into a dimly lit hallway. His booted feet crunched the wood splinters as he crossed the threshold.

Directly across from the open front door was a wide, grand staircase that rose and swept up and over to the right. A balcony railing lined the stairs. He noted a few closed doors atop the open air hallway. A large blackened iron chandelier hung from a long steel chain, swaying gently in the warm air. Blood red candles sat unlit in their holders. He looked around the sparsely furnished front room. Dust was a thick coverlet.

Denis frowned. If this was an example of the rest of the house, it wasn't exactly worth insuring, let alone any inspection. More likely in need of a maid. He shook his head and wondered why the owner had bothered calling his company. He struggled to remember. *What was it his supervisor had said? Damn it.* All he could recall was a holding company in New Jersey on the investigation order.

His silent reverie was interrupted as footsteps echoed down to Denis from above.

Shite.

"Who are you?" a deep voice demanded. A tall, black garbed figure materialized at the top of the stairs. Deep shadow obscured his face but Denis could see it leaning forward to peer at the shattered doorway. "What are you doing?" The figure started down the stairs.

Denis could now see this was a man dressed in black trousers and tunic. Some form of cloak was wrapped around his shoulders. His shaven head was crowned by a black skullcap. His eyes gleamed wickedly.

Denis held up his empty hand. "Easy friend, I'm here to-"

The man drew forth something from his side and launched it in one smooth motion.

That something whizzed a mere inch from Denis' face.

Thunk.

A long, thin blade quivered in the door frame. He blanched.

Son of a bitch. Next one probably has my name on it.

The man drew forth another dagger and growled a phrase in a language Denis did not recognize. This evil-looking black blade was serrated along one edge, shorter than the first but no less deadly. The cloaked man started quickly down the stairs, holding the weapon low.

Denis took up a stance, crouching slightly. He brought the Dragoon up and sighted the approaching madman. "Okay, put the knife down, boyo," he bellowed, as he cocked the hammer.

The man's eyes were a fever glow of fanaticism. Spittle flew as he cursed Denis vehemently and charged downward across the last few steps, knife now raised high.

Mad son of a bitch. He's not stopping.

A little closer. Wait for it.

Denis drew himself up, took one step back and held up his free hand in a stopping motion as he pulled the trigger. The Dragoon roared and the bullet caught the black garbed cultist square and point blank in the chest. Arms spread wide, he flew backward in a spray of blood as the force of the .44 caliber bullet ripped the life from his body. He landed heavily, sprawled at the bottom of the stairs. The knife tumbled from a lifeless grip and clattered on the hardwood floor.

Denis watched, sickened, as blood seeped from beneath the shattered body, spreading out across the floor in a slowly widening, crimson pool.

A thin, blue-white cloud of gun-smoke hung in the air like a vaporous ghost.

Denis expelled the breath he had been holding just as the sky above thundered with those ancient words. The house shuddered and rocked under the power. He clutched at the door frame.

DEES MEES....

What the hell is that?!

As if in answer to his unvoiced question, a girl's screams pierced the air, mixing with the thundering bass of that chant.

The fear dropped away from him and spurred him to motion. He gripped the Dragoon reassuringly as he made his way toward the back of the house in search of the stairs downward.

A gun-shot rang out above the black robed figure's head.

Only for a moment did he wonder who the interloper might be. His servant, Maxwell, obviously had met his end. He shrugged. No matter. It would soon be over. He turned back to the altar and began, ignoring the girl's frantic, terror stricken screaming.

He reached a hand down to her face, almost tenderly, to remove a sweaty strand of hair.

Repulsed, she pulled away from him, turning her face and whimpering as she strained at her bindings.

She would be silenced soon enough. He stood straight and tall before the altar, arms spread wide and head raised toward the sky, as he softly spoke the eldritch words of summoning. He listened rapturously as they were echoed and amplified above in the heavens.

"ENTIMAUS—"

The last word cracked the aether and he began the chant again, the echoes layering and harmonizing the ancient words.

His excitement mounted as each recital ripped the veil between worlds open wider. He pulled a breath and began once again, a small, tight smile on his lips as he mouthed the words.

The earth trembled and heaved. The doorway was opening!

They flowed from his lips, this chant that was forever burned into his memory and emblazoned in bright letters across the landscape of his mind.

Still chanting, he turned his attention to the altar and the bound girl upon it. She was weeping and straining against the chains that bound her.

"Please—" she begged, pulling at her bindings.

Cold metal held her fast.

Keeping up his chanting, he caught her gaze and slowly shook his head.

She struggled harder. "Stop it! Why are you doing this?" She twisted. "Let me go!"

Denis flung back the kitchen door and searched frantically about the darkened, empty room.

Goddamn basement door has to be around here somewhere. These houses are all the same.

His eyes settled on a spot near the window and wall. He checked the window. Completely blackened by whatever was covering the building. Shadowy shapes flowed across the panes of glass, as if the window was being buffeted by a murder of crows.

He made his way towards the corner of the room next to a series of tall cabinets. A narrow door, painted the same color as the wall greeted him.

Another frenzied cry reached up to him from below.

He swapped a fresh cylinder into the Dragoon. He briefly contemplated adding the shoulder stock but opted against it. *Probably going to be close quarters.* He spun the fresh cylinder once and listened as it clicked into place.

Satisfied, he reached for the door handle.

The thundering words rang out again and again, a chanting chorus of summoning. People screamed and ran for cover as the skies continued to blacken.

Niko ran. He dodged the frightened people the best he could and thrust aside those he could not. Most took one look at his flapping coat and ominous weapon and melted aside. The constabulary, demanding him to "Stop!" and blowing their whistles, attempted to apprehend him but could not keep up to his loping swiftness. In his head, Niko apologized profusely to them all as he left them behind, winded and confounded. He was certain that if they knew the circumstances, they would be following, not chasing him.

Alas, for there was no time to explain, nor was there any assurance of believability.

So on he ran.

The street he ran down grew more deserted the further he traveled until there was not a single pedestrian to be seen. The sky above the end of this next street was darkened by a whirlwind of clouds.

Lightning flashed deep within this chaos, illuminating the houses below it. Shadows were heavy and the last house on the corner was completely covered with the moving mass of them, as if alive.

He lowered the dark goggles and settled them over his eyes. Here the aural compass would not suffice. He needed to view the chaos with his eyes. The world before him darkened, but the shadow covered house was ablaze with alternating lights of electric blue and sickly green.

The material world dropped away and Niko could now see the energy trails emanating within the building and from deep in the obscuring cloud mass. Reaching up with his free hand, he turned a small dial along the outer frame of his goggles. It clicked once. The pattern in the cloud changed and became less opaque.

He could now view what was transpiring within the unnatural cloud formations above the houses. A lump of sickly, brackish hued tentacles, much like an octopus, was pulsing, attempting to push its vast bulk through a huge dark hole in the sky. He watched this repulsive scene, dread building in his stomach. That dark void was a jagged slash against the blue summer sky. He thought he could see stars out beyond the tentacled horror.

He cursed. This was not good. Not good at all. He prayed that he would not have need of the book. He touched his side where the old book rode in the hidden pocket, then looked over his rifle quickly once more. He pushed down that dread before it had chance to engulf him. For some reason, his brother's care-free, laughing face came to him in that moment, lending him a courage that he could feel. His mind flashed back to those younger days when Dane and he would stay up late, far into the night, talking of the grand plans for the future they would both share. Niko smiled and felt his spirit lighten. His brother was there beside him then, urging him on.

This was it.

Six

The chanting continued.

Denis stepped forward and descended as quickly as he dared. What fresh hell was he about to plunge into? He struggled to contain the insidious tendrils of growing fear and horror. He kept one thought on the girl's safety and one on his own need for iron courage.

The house trembled and shook, sending him jumping forward to grab the hand rail of the heaving basement stairs. He managed to save himself from a tumble downward. Strange colored lights were flashing upward from below. The air felt thicker here and it was a struggle to breathe. His heart thudded in his chest and his palms were slick on the railing. He wiped them on his pants.

Jesus Christ. Get a hold of yourself, Denis lad. He shook his head with a deliberate effort as he tried to keep a grip on his sanity. He felt like he was slipping again. He squeezed his eyes shut as flashes of muzzle fire and the crashing shatter of cannon fire swept through his mind. Battlefield slaughter played across the landscape of his closed eyelids.

The girl's screams grew more frantic.

Shite! Move it!

He descended the stairs as quickly as he could, trying not to trip and kill himself before he could execute a rescue.

The scene before him was cut straight out of a nightmare, and he had walked directly into the middle of it.

He stood in place on the bottom stair step frozen, pistol held securely in one hand, the other gripping the railing in an effort to keep himself upright. Time seemed to slow down as he scanned the lower level of the house. Cellar wasn't quite the right word because the upper end of the area was carved away into the earth, extending the surface area by about 20 or so feet. It was dressed out with field-stone and supported in places with several mortared brick pillars. An intricately carved arch demarcated the line between the two rooms. The keystone of this arch displayed some sort of odd line drawing, the shape of what appeared to be an eye bisected by a bolt of lightning, like ancient cave drawings he had seen in a museum once.

Nestled within this cave-like extension, a massive black basalt altar squatted like a torpid toad. Carved with runes and sigils, it exuded an air of watchful anticipatory power. A young girl was manacled and chained to the top of this repulsive piece of rock. Her pale flesh was a sharp contrast against the black stone.

Another dark robed figure stood before the altar, an evil looking dagger held in one outstretched hand, the fingers of which ended in sharpened, black-tipped nails. The other hand was clenched in a fist. The figure was chanting, the words projected skyward and amplified.

Denis blinked. The sickly green aura surrounding the robed being bordered on palpable and he swallowed the foul taste welling up in his mouth.

Both the girl and the figure turned their heads towards Denis.

She thrashed in her bindings. "Sweet Jesus, help me!" She screamed, her terror stricken eyes pleading with him.

He took a step forward, raising the Dragoon. *This is insane.*

Niko gave the swirling mass surrounding the house only a brief moment of inspection. Although this was a new phenomenon, he did not wish to linger in observation. A wave of exhaustion swept over him as the sedative-like by product effect of the chanted ritual tugged at his consciousness.

Wincing, he shook his head.

The steps up to the shattered front door beckoned. He set his shoulders and settled the rifle's grip in his hand.

He eyed the destruction of the door as he climbed the steps, his footsteps sounded hollow in the thick, warm air. His hand absently twisted and clenched the rubber grip.

Thunderous words echoed in waves from the sky, assaulting his ears and threatening his sanity. Startled, he jerked his head upward as those eldritch words rang clear and insistent, vibrating deep inside his chest and sinking into bone.

Muttering a curse in Serbian, he leaned against the door jam and flipped open his coat. He shook his head and drew forth the book, gazing with reluctant satisfaction at its cover. The metal sigil glowed a deep blue.

"Hazel, my dear. It looks like I do indeed have need of your book." He thanked the open-minded young librarian.

Cradling the rifle in the crook of his arm, he freed his weapon hand to flip through the parchment pages. He tried to ignore the vast pounding of the incantation as it reverberated from the aether. He closed his eyes, letting his mind clear. One by one he felt through the dry pages until the tell-tale twitch in his fingers gave away the proper verse.

There! He scanned the stanza once, quickly acquainting himself with the ancient words, then returned to the beginning. Thunder rumbled again and something in that morass of hell-spawned clouds growled. He looked up, grimly steeling himself as his thumb book-marked the page. He entered the darkened maw of the brownstone.

The air was heavy and thick.

Denis held his weapon steady despite the terror gripping his stomach. He gritted his teeth and struggled to breathe.

"Drop that dagger and let the lady go!" he demanded with clenched jaw as his mind struggled to process what was going on down here.

The eyes of the robed man narrowed to slits as he lowered his clenched fist. The dagger gleamed wickedly in the candlelight.

Denis pushed down his fear and willed himself forward another step. His heart was a pounding drum in his chest but his weapon arm was a rigid plank. He sighted down the barrel.

Without missing a beat, the man halted his chanting, letting the reverberating echoes keep the summoning words alive.

"Idiot." he said, then spat out a hissing string of unintelligible words as he flung out his free hand, palm up, at the same time Denis pulled the trigger.

In the time he took to blink, the Dragoon roared, and Denis flew backward, hitting the opposite wall.

Denis likened the experience to being thrown from the resulting force of a too close artillery blast. That same over-sized hand simultaneously slamming into and lifting him up as it launched him several yards into the air. It was not something he expected to relive again.

The shot from the Dragoon had gone wide, missing the black figure. The robed man laughed wickedly and continued his chanting where he had left off then lowered the dagger toward the heart of the struggling young girl.

Denis' shoulder was on fire and he felt nauseous. He shook his head, trying to blink away the stars. He rolled over, ears ringing with a bell toll. He looked down to see his hand was still tight around the weapon's handle. Somehow, he had managed to maintain his grip on the Dragoon.

He had to get up.

As Denis lifted himself off the stone floor, an explosion from above rocked the house. Timber and stone shrieked in protest, mixing with the screams of the girl. He dropped flat and instinctively covered his face and head.

From above them another voice rang out, strong, clear, and with what sounded like a retort or defiant counter chant. The force of these new words pushed against the power of the eldritch summoning. The air was a hot band of energy, crackling and spitting streams of blue and green electricity into the air like hissing snakes.

Robes flapping, the man stumbled, cursing.

The floor heaved sending dust and dirt sifting down upon them.

Denis winced, coughing dust, and pushed himself up, taking aim at the figure once more. There was absolutely no way he could miss this shot.

His head was an anvil and the girl's cries of helpless terror were the hammer.

Focusing, he noticed a small statue, grotesquely evil, at the foot of the altar and glowing with hunger as if in anticipation of a tasty meal. It pulsed with a sickly green inner light, and seemed to Denis as if it was drawing breath.

The robed man had regained his footing and was now wielding the dagger over the girl. A sense of urgency was evident in his movement. With a taloned hand he roughly grabbed and wrenched her head back by the hair, frantically resuming the chant, as he positioned the dagger for the sacrificial stroke.

The young girl heaved her body against the chains.

The robed man tensed and the dagger plunged downward.

Denis pulled the trigger twice.

His aim was true. The .44 slugs caught the man in the upper chest and spun him around, sending him staggering backward several paces, the dagger flying from his grasp, as he lost his footing and toppled over.

The statue's glow dimmed perceptibly.

Above them, the dying echoes of the summoning chant were overwhelmed by the new voice.

Something skyward was not too pleased with this new development. A deep bellow full of anguish followed the arrival of this new voice.

The black robed man echoed his frustration with a hideous scream.

What the hell? Astonished, Denis watched as the man righted himself, debris falling from the deep folds in the robe, apparently unharmed by the bullets lodged in his body.

He gave a wet cough and pushed back the hood to reveal a pale, long haired, weasel faced man, eyes feverishly bright and awash in madness, with lips drawn back in a snarl and flecked with white froth.

"You meddlesome bastard." He winced and growled through clenched teeth. Limping slightly, he advanced on Denis, cursing.

The echoing chorus of the new chant faded away.

Another explosion from upstairs rocked the house. The cellar ceiling rained splinters of wood and stone down upon them all. A thick cloud of dust kicked up, plunging the already dim room into deeper shadow.

Shite. As Denis rose, something slammed into the cellar door frame and upper stairwell with enough force to rattle his teeth. He could hear the shriek of metal. A faint odor filled the opaque air, the door now lay in a crumpled heap of charred and splintered wood at the bottom of the steps.

He struggled to his feet and backed up, bringing the Dragoon to bear on the black robed fanatic. He peered into the gloom and could just make out the silhouette against the fitful candlelight from the altar.

The black robed man drew himself up and muttered something in that harsh, ancient language. Denis could now see the man's aura glowing that sickly green again. He felt the power emanating off of him. Denis' eyes darted about the room. His back against the wall, he wasn't sure what he could do now. No other way out that he could see. Slow him down enough to get the girl and flee?

That would have to do.

"You already know that weapon is useless, you pathetic mortal slug." The voice slithered with contempt across the emptiness between them. Denis watched him take a limping step forward.

He frowned. "Probably" he admitted, the Dragoon's hammer made a solid click as he thumbed it back. "But, I'm thinking your little shindig here has been ruined, at least."

The black robed man laughed and raised his arm.

Denis sighted on his chest and pulled the trigger.

The world erupted in a cascade of bluish-white light.

For the third time that day Denis found himself flat out on the floor. The stone was refreshingly cold against his cheek. It felt good. Perhaps he should just stay here. Colored stars swam across his vision. He blinked rapidly, trying to banish them as he lifted his head to survey the damage.

What the hell was that anyway?

The cellar was a chaotic mess of stone and fallen timber. He lay sprawled several feet from where he had been standing. He coughed and looked around for the black robed man.

Nothing.

The silhouette of a man emerged out of the smoky haze. At first, Denis thought it was the black robed figure until he noticed the long coat flapping. He lifted himself on one arm and looked up as a slender hand reached down to him.

"Take my hand. We must act quickly!" The voice was strong and carried a hint of foreign lands.

Denis grabbed for the stranger's hand and levered himself up, wincing in pain as he did so. His whole body felt like one large patch of road that had been trampled over by a herd of cattle.

"Thanks," he grunted, standing straight. He stretched his back and eyed the strange weapon in the new comer's hand and noted his long coat, suit, and goggles.

His eyes widened and he grabbed his arm.

"Wait a minute!" he said, practically yelling. "It's you - from the street, back at the coffee house - outside!" he faltered, stumbling over his words.

The young man smiled at him, then turned toward the altar and the chained form of the young girl. "Yes, I remember you there. I thought I might be seeing you again." He said over his shoulder.

Denis stared at him.

He continued walking and added, "Admittedly, just not this soon." He shrugged. "No matter." He waved a hand at Denis. "Nikola Tesla, at your service, my friend." He turned at the waist to take in the room and gestured for Denis. "And now we must make haste and finish this." He pointed down to the girl. "We must see to this young lady." He quickly made his way over toward the grotto.

Denis blinked, still rather stunned from ordeal. "Yes, of course." He shook his head to clear it as he hurried over to Niko and the girl.

Spying his gun en route he stooped quickly to scoop it up. "My name is Denis Malone." He said.

"Well met, Denis Malone." Niko replied.

"What is...was this?" Denis asked as he joined Niko at the altar. "What the hell was that thing in the sky? Sounded like an animal." He looked at the spot where the black robed, weasel face man had stood. "And what the hell happened to that black robed jackass?" He demanded, holstering his weapon, and nodded at the empty space before him.

Niko bent his six foot plus frame over the altar and lifted the girl's manacled arm. "So many questions, my friend." He checked the girl's pulse. "The explanation to what has occurred here will take much time. Time we do not have." Satisfied, he set the girl's arm down and looked up at Denis. "Please" he gestured to the girl. "She is alive and we must free her."

Denis looked at the manacles and chains trapping her limbs and snorted. "Yea, but with what?" He spread his arms wide. "I forgot to pack my bolt cutters this morning."

Niko snorted. "We might find something if we look about." He lifted a manacled arm to show him the keyhole. "Perhaps a key?" he asked with raised eyebrow.

"That would be too easy." Denis mumbled. His eyes frantically searched the floor and walls near the altar. Nothing.

Two flameless candles sat upon a small intact wooden table near the back wall. He ran over to check, his eyes frantically darting about the wall and floor. There! Hanging from a rusty iron hook set in the wall almost at eye level, was a key.

"Well, what do you know?" he said, grabbing them. He rushed back to the altar and began unlocking manacles. "So, how about it, kid." He asked, freeing the girl's legs. "Going to tell me who that was?" He moved to unlock a wrist, then stopped. "What the hell are you doing down there?" He asked looking down at Niko.

The young man talked as he knelt on the floor, examining a small square box about the size of an alarm clock which he had produced from within the depths of his coat. "Please, Denis, you must take care of the girl." He said. "The stairs are unstable, but intact." He nodded to himself and twisted a dial. It clicked as he advanced it several turns. "Go, my friend." He smiled up at Denis reassuringly. "I shall be along shortly."

Denis was about to argue when the girl began to stir. He went back to unlocking the locks on her wrists. He lightly tapped her face with the back of his hand. "Little lady, time to get the hell out of here."

Her eyes fluttered open and her eyes widened. Flustered and frightened she thrashed and twisted about. "What?" She began to cry.

Denis removed his coat and wrapped it about her shoulders. "Shh, little lady it's okay, you're safe now," he assured her with soft words.

She let out a choked sob and fell against his shoulder. He could feel her quivering body through the coat. He gathered her up as gently as he could, lifting her against his chest. She was as light as a fawn and just as fragile. Denis held her close, whispering comforting words, as he started for the scorched stairs.

Niko was clearing a space in the center of the room. He brushed away dirt and rubble and nodded at Denis with approval. "Wait for me at the end of this street. I shall be along as quickly as I may." He laughed to himself. "I have no desire to linger longer than is necessary."

Denis let out a breath. "That works fine with me." He started up the stairs testing the first step. It held their weight. He grunted. "Hopefully the carriage and Mildred are still there," he muttered to himself. Halfway up he called down to Niko. "Good luck, Nikola."

"Call me Niko." He was out of view but Denis could hear the smile on the young man's face.

He shook his head and rose up to the top landing. He navigated the tumbled kitchen. "That kid is either really crazy or exceptionally brilliant." He mumbled into the girl's hair as he moved through the foyer and toward the front door.

Niko knelt amid the rubble of the shattered cellar and closed his eyes. Images splashed across the canvas in his mind. Piece by piece, they assembled, and he could see how his invention would work in reality. It was always thus. Smiling to himself, he opened his eyes and scanned the rubble strewn floor, making a few calculations. He moved the Resonator several inches to the right and adjusted the controls on the face of the little box accordingly.

A flickering shadow hovered on the periphery of his vision and the air grew colder. He whipped his head toward the elusive shape.

Nothing. Turning back, he toggled a small red switch. A red light glowed like a ruby. The box emitted a deep hum as it came to life, shuddering once, then giving forth a rumble that belied its size.

The ground began to vibrate in slow waves, each second a pulse rippled out.

"Are you sure you know what you're doing, little brother?" A voice whispered in his ear.

Dane.

Sudden anxiety gripped his chest like a vise. "Yes, yes!" Niko rose to his feet. "I've made all the proper calculations and only this building will fall." He shouldered his rifle. "The doorway to our world must be closed!"

Niko felt a hand on his arm, a soft touch, familiar and comforting. He thought he could sense Danes presence. "That's not what I meant, little brother."

"Dane, there isn't time! And I have to make this right!" he cried, running toward the stairs.

The ground pulsed and heaved.

He climbed the steps two at a time. The vibrations were gaining in strength, building on the one before it, causing the walls of the cellar to crack and tremble. The house groaned in protest and the bottom half of the stairs fell inward with a crash.

"Niko, it's not your fault." Dane's sad voice echoed in his head one last time as he threw himself through the shattered doorway.

The floor beneath Denis began to vibrate ever so lightly. He could feel it through his legs like a swarm of bees. He winced and moved faster, holding the girl tight to his chest.

"Shite, let's hope that's Niko," he muttered frantically, as he ran through the house.

His legs had that dull ache like when he sat too long with them crossed and they fell numb.

The shadow creatures were gone. The broken front door creaked quietly in the early summer breeze. This space was just a sad, forlorn empty house now.

He crossed the lintel.

The air was sweet, warm and peacefully quiet. He paused on the steps, taking slow, deep breaths, and gazed at the blue sky. The clouds were gone and the sun was strong and warm on his face. Smiling, Denis descended the stairs, careful not to disturb the girl too much, and headed up the street to where the carriage was still waiting.

Eager to be away from the horror, he strode quickly away from the shaking house.

Pushing his cap up, the cabbie watched as they made their way up the street. He scratched his head, and looked at them in amazement.

Denis matched his look and shook his head. "Still here," he noted.

The cabbie barked a laugh. "Not for lack of tryin', but my four-legged friend here was too frightened to move and I was not about to leave 'er." He patted Mildred's rump fondly. "We've been through a lot."

Mildred stood shivering but stoic in her harness. She dipped her head as if nodding.

Denis snorted. "Then you saw all that?" he said, jerking his head back in the direction of the house.

The cabbie nodded wild eyed. "Madness! There was sumpin' in that cloud, all screaming and yellin' like." He shook his head, waving a hand up in the air above the houses. "Then there was voices and explosions, and -" his voice trailed off.

Denis said nothing as he approached the carriage door.

"So, what in all the nine hells was all 'o that?!" he demanded then pointed to the girl in Denis' arms. "She okay, captain?

"Yes, and stop calling me captain, I was a sergeant." He moved toward the carriage seat. "Help me," he grunted. "Get that door open!"

"Huh - oh, sorry." The cabbie responded and moved quickly to open the door. "Should'a thought of that me-self."

Denis moved to settle the girl in the seat. "Thanks." He made sure his coat was covering her. "We have to wait, we have one more passenger," he said looking back down the block.

The cabbie gave him a quizzical look then shrugged. "If you say so," he conceded. He moved to untie the horse, then stopped, a frown forming on his face. "What is that?"

Denis could feel it too.

The ground was vibrating, a low consistent rumble that pushed out like a rippling wave. It was emanating from the corner house.

Suddenly Mildred neighed, snorting and bucking wildly as the street heaved and shifted. Both the cabbie and Denis reached out grabbing the carriage for support.

"What now?!" the cabbie shouted as he clutched the side of the foot-board.

As if in answer to the question, there was a shriek of ripping wood and grinding stone as the house collapsed, sliding and slithering in upon itself. A thick cloud of dirt and debris rolled slowly outward and up the street.

Denis stared wide eyed in horror.

"Shite! Niko." he said in a strained whisper.

"Someone still in there, captain?"

"Damn. I'm afraid the other passenger we were waiting for was still in that house." Denis felt sick to his stomach. He had only just met the young man, but no one deserved that, especially after what he just accomplished.

The dust cloud was slowly settling and starting to dissipate.

"Look!" the cabbie cried out.

Denis looked up. "Well, I'll be damned."

From out of the settling debris cloud they could just make out the silhouette of a limping figure. It was Niko. His face was coated with dirt and grime and his wide grin was a bright beacon as he waved to them, tiredly, but with triumph.

Denis was shaking his head in wonder as Niko approached and clapped Denis on the shoulder, then looked over to the cabbie. "It's over for now. Let's go, shall we?"

"Ya don't have to tell me twice," the cabbie said, vaulting into the driver seat.

Denis frowned. "What the hell does 'over for now' mean, exactly?" he asked lightly.

Niko remained silent as he pulled himself wearily up into the carriage. He sat down heavily with a sigh next to the unconscious girl.

Denis followed him and busied himself settling the girl against his side as he propped her up with one arm around her shoulders. He was acutely conscious of her nakedness underneath the coat. He pushed those thoughts away and looked over the girl's head to Niko who was sitting with his head back and his eyes closed.

There was a flap and flutter of wings as something white arrowed from the sky to land upon Niko's shoulder. He opened one eye as he turned his head slightly to regard the snow white pigeon. Its feathers seemed illuminated from within and incandescently bright, in sharp contrast with Niko's dark hair. The bird's head swiveled and its coal black eyes met Niko's. They scrutinized each other with a calmness that Denis found unnerving.

Denis, with eyebrows raised, pointed. "There's a pigeon on your shoulder," he said unnecessarily. "In case you missed it, what with all the chaos."

Niko did not respond but smiled, nodded knowingly, and closed his eyes again, ignoring both Denis and his new, feathered friend.

Denis shot him an irritated look. *Damn it. Okay, rest for now, but soon you're going to be answering a ship's ton of questions my strange friend.*

"Let's get out of here," he said out loud, kicking the carriage seat back.

The cabbie nodded and flicked the reigns as he made to turn the carriage around.

He cleared his throat meaningfully. "Now, captain, let's see. About your fare—"

About the Author

Vincent J. LaRosa resides in Southern New Jersey. When not working full-time as a computer geek he can be found enjoying the beauty of the NJ Pinelands and thinking up his next story. This is his first book.

Made in the USA
Las Vegas, NV
18 September 2022